Transform

Your

Sex Life

Complete guide to explore your fantasies
with incredible experiences, sex
positions for couples.
Discover incredible sex for men and
women.
Transform your marriage for good.

Patrick Rosales

Additionally, the information in the following pages is intended only for informational purposes and should thus be thought of as universal. As befitting its nature, it is presented without assurance regarding its prolonged validity or interim quality. Trademarks that are mentioned are done without written consent and can in no way be considered an endorsement from the trademark holder.

TABLE OF CONTENT

INTRODUCTION

Sex is not a rocket science and you need to keep improving your skills at it If you want to **KEEP TRANSFORMING YOUR SEX LIFE.** Good sex is a foundation for long term relationship and by spicing up your sex life; you can live a happy married life forever.

If you've been married for like 2 years and look back, you'll find that your relationship has changed a lot from the time you got married. Your sex life was great then and now it is not that spicy. If your passion for sex is fading then you need a quick transformation.

It is a simple truth that having a better sex life for a couple can make them love each other more. It will be hard to stay in a relationship where there is no sex. Sex is actually the answer to many problems that are affecting us nowadays.

Recent studies show that many married couples have less and less sex when they grow old. Lack of sexual desires or have almost non-existent sex life usually is the main cause why marriages do not work out.

As you may know, people who can enjoy better sex live longer, happier, and healthier life. This is because sex is one of the best sports created by God to us. Having a healthier sex life sometimes is just better than swimming 20 laps daily.

Believe or not? When someone is able to have healthier sex regularly, their skin colors glow as a sign that they are satisfied and enjoy with their life. This also makes them become more successful in other aspects of life such as their work careers.

When someone cannot have sex, it may lead to mild depression cases and they may become introverts. That is why more and more people are coming up with answers to boost their sex drives. A couple should always ensure that they keep the fire burning in their relationship.

Whenever you find that you or your partner have a difficulty in having sex, admit it. Nothing wrong by admitting you both have a problem in your sex life.

It remains a fact that the relationships last for a long time for couples who can maintain and enjoy their better sex life. Whenever they have encountered any problems in their life, they can and will stick together to face the harshness in life as one.

CHAPTER ONE

INTRODUCTION TO REAL SEX LIFE

"REAL" SEX

Most couples already engage in some form of outercourse such as kissing, snuggling and foreplay. However, they may find they can achieve better sex if they make outercourse a more important or prominent part of their sexual activities.

For most people, "having sex" means inserting the penis into the vagina - and it's easy to see why. But people often experience better sex if they take a broader view of the activity. When the goal is to achieve intimate bonding through physical contact, the couple can find satisfaction in extending the amount of outercourse before or after penetration - or even by not making penetration the ultimate goal of the activity.

Would you like to improve that percentage? Are you a baby boomer who is heading into the final third and would like to make these days filled with sexual sunshine? Are you younger and want to do everything you can to make sure that the flame burns eternal?
Yes, it is true. You can have passionate sex for a lifetime. It's easy, it's fun, and it's free!

So what's the secret? The secret is love. Just about everyone wants love, but who thinks about giving it? If you can keep your intention, your focus, and your actions on giving love, you can have great sex with one person for a lifetime. The big question is, what does it mean to give love?

- **Security**

Everybody wants someone who is dependable, who shows up, who can be trusted, and does what they say. A dangerous relationship can be very hot for a while, but eventually, a relationship with someone who doesn't make you feel safe gets ugly. And it gets boring for all your friends who have to listen to you complain about a bad relationship you don't get out of. When our bodies believe that they are in danger, the last thing they want to do is open, surrender, and let go.

- **Connection**

The most important part of giving love is cultivating authentic connection. Authentic connection comes from caring contact and communication. Be open, honest, and considerate in communication. Listen, understand, and empathize. This doesn't mean that sexy relationships are without conflict. A relationship without conflict has no heat! It is about real engagement with basic respect for your partner. If you have a conflict, let the guiding motivation be to respond, repair, and resolve rather than react and attack.

- **Self-Care**

Take care of your temple, otherwise known as your body. That's the part of you that has sex after all. Eat well, get off substances, exercise. If you want to want to have sex, if you want all the parts to work, and if you want to turn on your partner - especially as you are visited by the ravages of time - you better take care of yourself.

One part of that temple is your brain. That needs to be worked on also if you want to have good sex. Live a full, interesting life. If you're boring, your sex will be, too.

- **Appreciate**

If you want to be turned on, you've got to turn yourself on. If you want to turn on your partner, you've got to be turned on by them.

Find your partner's beauty. Savor them. Let yourself feel how incredible it is that you get to look at, smell, touch, and taste a naked human body.

Celebrate what you love about your partner. Instead of focusing on your negative judgments, think about what is great about your spouse. Tell your lover what you adore about them.

- **Attune**

Have sex be first about what you give, second about what you share, and third about what you get. Attune yourself to your partner's pleasure. By focusing on their responsiveness, you can bring them to the ultimate heights of pleasure. If you do that, your partner will want to have sex with you till you die.

- **Sense**

Learn about your own body's responsiveness. Pay attention to what feels good to you. As Sister Wendy said, why would God give you a toy and not want you to play with it? If you can figure out what feels good, you can find it with your partner. All too many people spend too much sex time worrying how they look, worrying what the other person is thinking, evaluating what is going on. Get out of your head and into your senses.

- **Be Passionate**

Passion is the ability to put all of yourself into what you are doing with utter abandon. It is being able to jump off the cliff with no parachute and fully enjoy the ride down. Breathe, smile, look into your partner's eyes. Express yourself completely. Let yourself show all of your heart.

- **Practice**

Have sex. Have as much sex as you can get. You and your partner will be dead soon, and unless you believe in reincarnation or some kinky heaven, this is going to be your one chance in all of eternity to get it on. There's always an excuse not to have sex. If you need an excuse to have it, how about this one: you're going to be old and then dead very soon. Research shows that the more we practice something, the better we get. Try new stuff and keep doing it till you get it right. Be willing to learn from your partner. Ask your partner for directions and feedback, and don't get all sensitive if they ask for something different.

- **Create**

Sex is always the same, always different. Be in the moment. Be creative. Follow your impulse. Do it hard, soft, up, down, in, out. Follow your partner's rhythm. Expand your concept of sex. If you want to keep it interesting for a lifetime, you better be willing to try new spices.

HOW TO TAKE CONTROL OF YOUR SEX LIFE

How Is Your Sex Life?

Want to keep your libido sizzling? Maybe it does not need any more polishing. You have attained the honors in your sex life but wait until you hear these questions. They might awaken your senses. Little things you say or do tell a lot about the level of your sex life and thus the success of your relationship. Healthy sex life is the real meaning of a good marriage or any other relationship whether long term or short term. You can be a king in bed if you test how your sex attitude is and maintain it or improve it. After a gruelling and hectic day, what do you feel like doing? having a bubble bath, enjoying a glass of wine or some serious undisturbed sleep?

If this is the case you need to know some facts maybe they can boost your libido. The hormones released during sex relieves headache and mild depression. Watching your favorite indicates you need some more sex awareness hence your libido is low. If you feel like going for games you must be having the best libido. That athletic body cannot allow you to sleep without having sex. The flow of blood is known to be good for circulation of sex hormones you will be yearning for more every day all the time. By the way, what would you rather do if you suddenly found some free thirty minutes out of your busy schedule? Get something down your stomach, do some online stock exchange transactions or lock the door for some quickie with a lover? Sex is fun and I know good sex life can give you fun do a lot of it.

Another important question to help you gauge your sex life: what do you focus on during sexual encounters?

If you usually think about the load of work you have to clear, it is so unfortunate. It is even worse if you focus on how your breasts are scarred or how your thighs are sagging. This shows that you are uncomfortable with your body and uncomfortable with sex too. This affects your sex life in a great way. Forget about it and concentrate on the pleasure you are giving or receiving. If your sex life is superb, you should be focused on the moans and screams from your partner.

If your sex life is good you will be innovative, ready for risks. This creates sexual excitements to amazing levels. What is your view on sex in the showers? Is it dangerous since it is slippery? No, that should not be the right attitude for exciting sex life.

It is even more funny if you look at it as water conservation since you are showering together. Life is not all about saving.

Your sex life is stunning if you look at it as the ultimate sexual fantasy which sends you over to the edge. What is your perfect description of your last time together? Were you glad since you finally crossed it off in your to-do-list? If it is so, your sex life is going down the drain if drastic measures are not taken but if you screamed until your neighbors complained you are doing fine.

LEARNING ABOUT PENETRATION POSITION FOR A BETTER SEX

In our society today, many men and women often wonder whether penis size is really important or not. Does size matter? If we look at it from other aspects, everything is larger today. Larger population, larger cars, larger salary; but what about larger penises?

Despite hearing the saying, "It's not how big, it is how you deal with it," the truth is that most male-female partnerships end up in the bin because of failure to meet the sexual requirements of the opposite sex.

Some women prefer men with larger penises. Of course, most women won't tell you that. As a guy, you want your women to enjoy sex as much as you do too, right?

A small penis that is, short and small in girth puts men in such an awkward position that many get embarrassed during sexual activity.

Even to undress alone during that moment is too much for some because time of reckoning has come unexpectedly. This psychological stress has to be fought from all angles and many must undergo counseling to restore their sexual esteem. It is a myth unfortunately with disastrous consequences yet many women don't even care about the size as long the job gets done well. For some, it is the girth that matters most as opposed to the length.

What is Penis Curve?

It is not abnormal to have a slight curvature in the penis. In fact, most men have their penises curved slightly towards one side. It is nothing out of the ordinary, and in most men, it does not hamper the man from performing penetrative sex. However, in some people, there is a condition called Peyronie's disease. Men suffering from this disease have very large curvatures of their penises, so much so that penetrative sex becomes a difficulty for them. It is in this case that penis curves need to be surgically corrected.

Any deviation of the male penis from the straight position can be termed as a penis curve. The penis is a highly flexible organ, and due to this, it can curve in any position. It can be tilted to the right or to the left, or even upwards and downwards. Even among people with penis curves, there are different extents of curvatures.

The human penis is about 5.5 to 7.5 inches long on an average when erect. Of course, there are men with penises on both sides of this scale. The main bulk of the penis is a spongy tissue called the corpus cavernosa. The corpus cavernosa contains two channels of spongy tissues which run through the length on both sides of the penis. In healthy men, both the channels of the spongy tissues grow equally and the penis becomes straight. However, if for some reason, one channel of the corpus cavernosa grows more than the other, then it would lead the penis to get inclined on the other side.

This generally occurs during injury. In men who suffer accidents on one side of the penis, the spongy tissues on that side may not grow properly. This would lead to a drop on the other side. Even wearing tight underwear may cause irreparable damage to the penis and cause it to gain an unnatural curve. Men who indulge in very hectic sexual intercourse could damage their penises. One example of this is the wrong use of the woman on top position. This position has the possibility of the penis coming out often and this could tear some of the ligaments. Anal sex is also responsible for penis curvatures.

REASONS WHY YOUR SEX LIFE MAKES A 180 DEGREE TURN FOR THE BETTER WITH A BIGGER PENIS

Does size matter? Can't I just learn different sex positions? Shouldn't I just increase foreplay? Isn't "how you use it" more important than size? These are all of the questions some men who have a smaller endowment tend to ask on a frequent basis. This is because they are trying to cope with having a smaller penis size. The bottom line is yes, size does matter, and yes, you could learn different sex positions, and yes, you could increase foreplay, and yes, you can improve your sex life by improving your skills with sex. However, if you have a bigger penis, then you are sure to turn your sex life around ENTIRELY.

Now, before I talk about those 20 reasons why being bigger will make your sex life better, I just wanted to talk to you about something real quick. Listen, if you want to get your penis bigger, please do it naturally. Please don't get suckered into thinking that taking pills (especially those dangerous ones made with Yohimbe), going in for surgery, or using some type of device is going to effectively enlarge your penis and improve its appearance. Those things do not work, they are way too dangerous, and way too over-priced. Also, with all the following amazing reasons why you should increase your size, please understand that it's not just having a longer penis that will make the following things happen. Your penis has to be long, thick, hard, and attractive looking. This can only happen with NATURAL enlargement. Natural enlargement lengthens your penis up to 9 inches long, thickens your manhood, makes your erections rock-hard, and will also increase your libido, your lasting power with sex, and more.

Alright, now with all of that said, here are 20 reasons why (broken down for YOU, for HER, and during sex) bigger is certainly better:

For You -

i. A bigger penis increases her desire to go oral...

One of the best things about having a larger endowment is that this usually causes women to feel more inclined to go oral. Even more so if you have an attractive looking penis (straight erection, hard, thick, long, and muscular looking). The only thing that gets's you an attractive looking penis is a 100% all natural enlargement method.

ii. Being large increases your confidence... and this will show before, during, and after sex...

When you have a bigger endowment, your alpha male swagger turns on at a very high rate. You don't become conceited, but you do become VERY confident that you know you are going to knock her stockings off!

iii. Your significant other is more likely to initiate sex for a change...

Ah, here is something that is probably new for most of us men! How about your significant other initiating sex for a change?! This is more than likely to happen if you have a penis that is sure to make her go wildly insane.

iv. The doggy style position is several times more sensual with a bigger penis (and this is mutual)!

The "doggy-style" position is a very popular position during sex and is one that men love the most. If you have a thick and long penis, then this position is going to be made even more intense for both you and her.

v. A bigger penis eliminates her dependency on sex toys or masturbating...

There is nothing more demoralizing than knowing your significant other is relying on sex toys to get her screaming orgasms! OUCH! Well, if you have a bigger manhood, you'll soon find those toys in the trash!

For Her -

vi. Flaccid size is made bigger and this alone can get women in the mood...

If you choose the right enlargement technique to get you a bigger endowment, not only do your erection size increase, so does your flaccid hanging size.

When women see that bulge in the pants or boxers, this REALLY turns her on. This is sort of like us men seeing very sexy cleavage or camel toe.

vii. The appearance of a commanding size (7-9 inches) turns her on...

When you are large and in charge, this really gets women turned on like crazy. And by the way, anything bigger than that usually scares the bejesus out of women! So don't worry about trying to get your size as big as some of that HUGE porn-stars! 7-9 inches is ideal.

viii. Nerve stimulation...

Her nerve endings inside her are better stimulated with a long and thick penis

ix. The clitoris...

Her clitoris is easily stimulated with a thicker penis rubbing on her vagina.

x. Thrusting...

Thrusting is more sensual for her when you have a bigger endowment.

-

xi. Rock-hard..

A harder penis feels good inside her instead of a soft or slightly hard erection. If you choose an effective enlargement method, you will also naturally increase blood circulation to your penile shaft. Because of this, not only will you increase the thickness of your manhood, you will also increase how hard your erections are as well.

xii. Her orgasms will reach "screaming-level"...

With being hard, thick, and long, you are several times more likely to cause her to reach a screaming orgasm. Making women SCREAM with an orgasm is very rewarding! Trust me on this!

xiii. Her "riding" you is way more intense for her (and this, of course, is mutual).

xiv. A big head is important as well...

Having a bigger penis head causes stimulating pressure on her nerve endings at the opening of her vagina. Increasing the size of your penis head is only done with a natural growth method by the way.

During Sex -

i. Endurance...

Since your PC muscle is stimulated with a natural enlargement method, you will be able to go for longer periods of time during sex.

ii. Stronger ejaculation...

Also, since your PC muscle is stimulated, your ejaculation will shoot out further.

iii. Longer lasting erections...

Due to more blood flow into your penile shaft, not only will your erections become firmer and bigger, but they will also last longer.

iv. More sex positions...

Having a bigger penis (such as 7-9 inches long) means you could do many difficult sex positions (such as doing it from the side).

v. Multiple orgasms for both partners...

For you, since you have better blood flow, you will be able to ejaculate more than once without that dreaded sore feeling. For her, well, I don't think I need to explain why she's going to be reaching orgasms several times!

vi. More satisfied after sex.

And lastly, with you having a bigger penis making sex explosive for you and certainly for her, you both will feel VERY satisfied after sex.

And the best natural enlargement option to bring about those 20 amazing benefits to your sex life is natural penis hand exercises.

DEEP PENETRATION POSITIONS - EXPLOSIVE ORGASM FOR BOTH OF YOU

Fortunately, you do not have to master the skill of a porn actor to satisfy your woman. There are few easy positions that allow deep penetration and erotic stimulation for both of you. Read out as we reveal the low down of the best deep penetration positions:

Important: Do Not Underestimate Foreplay!

Foreplay for men is everything that happens about 3 minutes before sex.-Dr. Louann Brizendine

If you view foreplay this way, then you are into a lot of troubles. According to experts, it takes minimum of 15 minutes of arousal time before a woman can reach orgasm. Foreplay is a key step to prepare her for lovemaking. It helps to release fluids from private areas to enhance sexual pleasure and orgasms. If you rush sex, she will have difficulties to achieve the big "O". Besides, she may feel uncomfortable with your penetration due to lack of moisture. There's nothing worse than a painful intercourse!

In a nutshell, please do not be stingy with foreplay. There are many ways to make her hot in foreplay, including hugging, oral sex, kissing, and sensual massage. The primary focus should be her pleasure.

DEEP PENETRATION POSITIONS

1. Lotus Position

In this position, you sit on bed with extended or crossed legs. She sits on your lap and places her hands on your shoulder. Then, she wraps her legs around your waist with moving up and down along your penis shaft.

Tip: As she is doing her job, try to squeeze your PC muscle as though you are doing Kegel exercise. It will exponentially intensify your orgasm!

2. Full Mast Position

It is the classical missionary position with a little twist. As she lies on her back, put her legs on your chest, then raise legs up to form a "L" shape in relation to her body. You kneel down in front of her and penetrate from front. This position allows deep thrusting and provides high level of sensation as it makes you feel "tight".

Tip: Instead of lying on bed, have her to lie on a table where her buttock is positioned at the edge. It will allow you to penetrate deeper and leave your hands free to fondle her body.

3. Cowgirl Position

Cowgirl position is a wonderful deep penetration position. It allows for deep thrusting and erotic stimulation. In a typical cowgirl position, you lie on your back while she sits on top of you to do all the work. She is in charge of the angle and speed of stimulation which equals maximum sensation for both of you. If your woman is conscious with body image, suggest reverse cowgirl position which she faces against you.

Tip: The up-and-down movement can be pretty tiring for her. You can have her to slightly bend forward and move back and forth. It requires less efforts from her and also increase chances of clitoral orgasm.

4. The Crab Embrace

In this position, couples lie down side by side and facing each other.

She puts her arms on your shoulder and a top leg on your waist. You lie between her legs as you go inside her from front. It's a superb position for incredible vaginal and clitoris arousal. Also, it allows you to last longer in bed.

1. **Modified Missionary Position**

In this position, her upper body lies on her back. Her lower body is vertical to form an "L" shape in relation to upper body. You penetrate her while allowing her to rest her legs on your shoulder. When she is getting aroused, bend her buttock forward a little. It will let you penetrate deeper.
Tip: put a big pillow under her to raise the position of buttock. It will exponentially increase the chances of multiple orgasms.

LEARNING THE POWER OF TICKING OVER DURING SEX

When it comes to sex, patience is a virtue. Unlike men, women do not have the ability to dive right into sex. She needs some warming up actions to get her into the mood. It is no secret that women like to be touched. Where and how you touch can have an effect on how soon she will reach orgasm.

Before you head south for the final assault, you have to start elsewhere. Here are some erogenous zones you can work on to pleasure her.

1. Face

She will love it when you touch her face. Caress her cheeks, ears and temples with gentle upward and outward strokes using your fingers. Using circular motions, you gently massage the center of her forehead and the bridge of her nose with your thumbs.

Move your hands gently upward and brush away the loose hair on both sides of her face. This gesture shows that you are considerate of her and make her feel closer to you. Run your fingers up through her hair and use the locks to tickle her face, neck and any part of the body which can be reached. Slow and light touching with the ends of her hair can both relax and tempt her.

2. Back

Treat her back as one long erogenous zone. Trace it with your fingertips from the back of her neck to her buttocks, lingering at any spot that produces a moan. Pay attention to the part of the back that meets the buttocks; which has a lot of nerve endings. Run your fingers lightly over this area without triggering the tickle reflex too much.

3. Buttocks

Many women expect you to grab their buttocks during sex and they want you to do it firmly.

To give her a surprising jolt of pleasure, lift and bring the buttock cheeks apart. You can gently slap on her buttocks and on the area you have just spanked, apply cold cream on it. This contrasting hot and cold sensation will make her whole body tingle with excitement.

4. Feet

They are packed with lots of nerve endings that some women claim can help them to reach orgasm just by having their feet rubbed. The key to a foot massage that does not make her feel ticklish is a firm touch. You should press with the right amount of pressure (too hard will cause pain, too light will tickle) to give her pleasure.

Add some lotion to your palms to help you glide along her feet. Gently massage the soles using your entire hands. Next focus on each toes separately, massaging and tugging as you go. Pay special to the middle toe, which some researchers believe, has a direct nerve connection to the genitals.

5. Any Parts Or Areas Of The Body That Can Be Folded

These are the often overlooked erogenous zones that can be found on the folds between the upper and lower arm, the back of the knees, the folds where the legs meet the trunk and the folds where the legs meet the feet (the arch). You can give these areas light kissing or caressing that will give her unexpected thrilling sensations.

6. Pubic area

Position yourself behind her, use one hand to cup her entire pubic area. Rest the heel of your palm on the hair-covered area, and then curl your fingers to use gentle back-and-forth and circular motion between the vaginal lips and over the clitoris. Start slowly and occasionally stop a while to keep her guessing and then increase your speed as she gets aroused.

You can use your other free hand to play with her nipples which have super sensitive nerves connected to the pleasure nerves in her clitoris and vagina. Therefore giving her simultaneous stimulation on these 2 areas can blow her mind.

7. Perineum

This is the area between the vaginal opening and anus. There are a lot of nerve endings in this area that respond well to light pressure or gentle stroking. If you can reach it, this is an area that is great to stimulate during thrusting. Use one or two fingers to apply moderate pressure on the perineum.

HOW TO TICKLE A MAN'S MIND IN A WAY WHICH MAKES HIM OBSESSED WITH YOU.

First, determine how obsessed you want him to be about you

It's all very well to want your man to be obsessed with you. But sometimes obsession can become dangerous when it reaches levels that are uncontrollable. A little harmless obsession that borders on deep commitment and love is just fine.

- **Stay Out Of Reach**

Go out of your way to attract your man. Let him have a good look at your beauty, charm and a good taste of your scintillating company. Then all you have to do is stay just out of reach. He will be crazy for you and long to catch you. This way he will be obsessed with your attractiveness and do all he can to conquer you.

- **Stay In Control Of The Situation**

In these circumstances, it is very important for one of you to be in control of the situation. Keep your head and don't go overboard in anything that you do. This way you can control the pace at which the relationship is going. The more confident and assured you are - the more he is going to be under your spell!

- **Make Him Always Want More Of You**

The easiest way to make him want you badly is to leave him wanting more. This will keep him coming back! Know when he has had enough of waiting and give in after a while, only to pull away again! This game if played cleverly will make him obsessed with you.

- **Keep Him In A State Of Anticipation**

Always make him wonder what you are going to do next. This way you will always be on his mind and he is going to look forward to being entertained by you. Being impulsive as well as spontaneous will make you different from all the other girls he has known before.

- **Stop Seeing Him Every Day**

Once he has seen how stimulating and exciting you are he will want to be with you every waking (and sleeping) moment! The trick is to keep away just enough for him to want you desperately. This feeling of loss when you are not around will prove that he is obsessed with you.

- **Pretend That You Are Pulling Away**

This is another way to make him become obsessed with you. He will want you to be solely his if you pretend that you are losing interest in him. A little bit of flirting and giving other guys attention will scare him and he will want to spirit you away!

COMMUNICATION - THE ART OF GOOD SEX BEGINS WITH COMMUNICATION

Good sex begins with communication. Certainly, communication is a foundation for every type of relationship. Whether it is between a working relationship, friendships, or our families, communication makes life easier and is the vehicle by which we fix the broken. When it comes to sex, communication has pretty much been taken out of the game for the past 10,000 years. Society teaches and conditions us to think that to talk about sex is a guilty obsession in any context.

The reluctance to talk comes from fear of rejection or that you will harm the other's feelings. But your partner may want to talk as well, but fears that they will be rejected or hurt you in turn. Even in a good and loving relationship where trust is important, sex is often a sensitive subject to most people. While difficult, creating an open dialogue about sex produces results that both can be happy about, resulting in a better relationship overall.

When you take the time to talk about your sex life in a clear, and honest way can greatly improve the intimacy in your relationship, giving the relationship a better chance at lasting.

1. Think Before You Speak.

Before you even think about talking about your sex life with your partner, you need to know what you actually want beforehand. In this process, you should want to discuss improving your sex life, to enjoy the sex you and your partner have more than you do now; not getting upset that he forgot to take out the trash last week. When you are sure that your intentions are positive and are focused on just the intimacy you share, devise a plan of all the things you'd like to discuss. You also need to keep in mind the feelings of your partner, and what exactly you truly want. Make a list if this makes things easier to organize and remember.

2. Ask The Right questions.

When you are being intimate, begin to touch your partner the way you normally do, but while you do so, ask them what they want: do you like it when I nibble on your neck?

Do you like it when I squeeze your nipples? Am I applying enough pressure to your clitoris? Is deep thrusting OK with you? Once they let you know what they enjoy in bed, please remember that these preferences will always stay the same; throughout the relationship, keep the conversation on sexual preferences an ongoing one. Each person in the relationship needs to be heard, you need to be honest on your part, and a good listener when your partner speaks up about their desires. It can put a damper on lovemaking when you have to answer a million questions while trying to be intimate; an even bigger damper is when you let your lover know what you want, only to have him end up forgetting.

3. Get In The Mood.

Pick when and where you would like to get intimate; where you both can be alone and free of distraction (at home is most likely best).

If you would like to increase the amount of sex you have, perhaps setting up the proper mood before seducing your lover; light candles and run a bath for the two of you, then go to them, kiss them, touch them.

By doing this, you are communicating to them that you want intimacy without even saying a single thing.

4. Keep Positive.

When you want to communicate to your partner about the things they do that you like or dislike, stick to telling them what they do well. It's a very sensitive subject when it comes to how a person makes love, none of us wants to hear that the things we thought we were doing well are actually not all that hot. When you tell them that it drives you mad when they nibble on your ear instead of telling them you hate when they lick your belly, they'll begin to focus on the things you tell them you really like.

5. Give Very Clear Instruction.

This is more or less a continuation on the last point where we want to keep criticism to a minimum (whether constructive or negative).
Tell your partner exactly what you would like to happen, and what you'd specifically like done to you.

Don't be clinical about it, but be clear; you can whisper something like, "look in my eyes while you unbutton my shirt," or, "when you kiss me, run your fingers down my torso," or even, "touch my breasts". I know you get it, it's simple but straightforward.

Doing this will get you what you desire, but it can also add a touch of eroticism by expressing what you want in words, being honest and vulnerable.

6. Talk Through Touch.

There are times when you won't actually need to talk to communicate what you want from your partner; you can very simply direct your lover with your hands to where you want to be touched, or what position you'd like to be in. You could even turn this into a game, neither of you are allowed to talk, you're only allowed to use your hands - and maybe some non-verbal sounds as they happen naturally - to help you communicate what you both want.

7. Use Positive Reinforcement.

When your lover does something you really love when you're being intimate, tell them!

Tell them that you love it when they do that, that what they just did was amazing; or you could always go the non-verbal route and moan about it.

Let them know when they're doing something good because everyone enjoys hearing what they're good at, that what they're making an effort at is paying off and giving you both pleasure. Everyone desires praise, and why not give it when it comes to sex?

8. Talk Dirty During Sex

Getting a little naughty and experimental in bed can have its perks. The key to having great sex is not even by having a perfect body or doing it all the time, learn how to talk dirty during sex. It's pretty simple (not to mention exciting!) Here are a few tricks to get her crazily turned on for you:

- **Call Her Name.** And make her call yours. Right in the middle of your lovemaking, it's quite an overwhelming feeling when your partner starts to call your name like a chant --- I can't exactly describe the feeling that's why you better try it to know what I mean. But I do assure you --- it's going to get you all fired up for round two.

- **Be Specific.** Don't just tell her it feels good --- be a little specific. Tell her you love it when she does this or does that --- or the way she does this or does that and so on. The more you become vocal with your feeling, the more she'll be glad to do exactly what you want her to.

- **Do As You Say.** Tell about your fantasies and then slowly try to make them all come true. Women tend to be more tuned in with their partners when you make them mentally stimulated at first. So when you tell her you've been wanting to kiss her this way, then follow it up right away with the kiss you want --- she'll be crying out your name in no time.

- **Breathe Heavy.** Getting physically intimate is a very strong moment for a couple, that's why you still need to communicate, even through sighs, groans and breathing. She can tell if you're tired, bored or taking pleasure with having sex with her. So express yourself!
- **Moan And Groan.** You may find this as a surprise but faint sounds do make us totally

turned on --- especially if it came from our partners during sex. Don't stop the urge of creating some noise during the deed --- it's actually one major thing to help you both reach the peak.

PLEASURABLE FEMALE SEXUAL POSITIONS

The climax is the entire point behind each and every sexual encounter taken part in by a woman or a man because when a man or a woman reaches an orgasm, he or she is overcome with an indescribable, pleasurable feeling beyond comparison. Fortunately, men usually do not have much difficulty achieving this awesome feeling; however, this is not the case for the majority of women.

For a woman to experience that type of pleasure in the bedroom, she needs to do and experience certain actions leading up to an orgasm, especially if she is trying to achieve multiple ones.

Of course, foreplay is a major part of helping a woman experience pleasure and orgasms without penetrating the vagina. But if a woman wants to climax during vaginal penetration, she needs to try certain sexual positions. The following details five of the most pleasurable female sexual positions, all of which are highly popular with many women.

The First Position--Missionary

In order for most women to experience an earth-shattering orgasm during sexual intercourse, they will often need their partner to penetrate them deeply. And when it comes to deep penetration, nothing beats the missionary sex position where the woman lays flat on her back while the man gets on top of her. To add an extra component to a woman's pleasure factor, her partner can use his fingertips to stimulate the clitoris.

The Second Position--Modified Missionary

Just as with the traditional missionary position, the modified missionary sex position allows the man to deeply penetrate the woman as well as let his shaft rub and stimulate her clitoris while he thrusts.

In order to pull this position off, the woman will place either one of her leg over her partner's shoulder so he can thrust from a side angle.

Getting Better Sex From The Position

And what are some ways to enliven the old missionary? These tips can help.

- Move up a bit. After successfully entering the vagina, a guy can move his torso forward a bit, placing his hips slightly higher than the woman's. This places the pubic bone in a position to grind pleasingly against a portion of the female anatomy that is particularly prone to pleasure. It may take a little experimenting to get the positioning just right - but many women think it's definitely worth it.

- Employ a press. After penetration, the male should move his legs outside the females, and the female should clamp her legs tight together. This vice-like action can provide strong new sensations to the penis and the vagina during thrusting.

- Go the pillow route. If a partner would like deeper penetration, this can be achieved with just a little assistance from a pillow. Place it under her posterior, thereby raising her hips higher and creating a new angle for penetration which generally allows the penis to thrust deeper into the vagina.

- Try a new location. Plain old missionary can lead to even better sex when it's employed in a new setting. If a couple always has sex in their bed, try it on the floor (with sufficient carpeting or padding for comfort). Or take it to a new room altogether and see what sex on the sofa, in the kitchen, or in the laundry room is like. Those with a high enough privacy fence might even want to take things into the backyard. But enjoying sex in a different location can make it a new experience.

The Third Position--Doggy Style

The doggy style sex position is highly effective for helping any woman achieve a great amount of pleasure and hopefully, a mind-blowing orgasm during a sexual encounter.

All a couple needs to do for this sex position is to have the woman bend over at the waist at a 90-degree angle or get on her hands and knees and arch her back.

The man will then enter the vagina from behind. Although it may seem the man has total control, the woman can actually assume control over the speed and power of her partner's thrusts.

The Fourth Position--Cowgirl

This sexual position can take a woman to heights of pleasure she has never experienced before if performed correctly. The cowgirl sex position lets the woman sit on top of the man and take over where and how her partner thrusts.

The Fifth Position--Modified Doggy Style

The last position in this article--the modified doggy style sex position--requires the woman to lay on her stomach, completely flat. Her partner will then position his pelvis to have it sit directly above her pelvis. Doing this allows the penis to hit her g-spot while still letting the man be able to reach her clitoris for extra stimulation.

FEMALE EJACULATION - HOW TO GUSH, SQUIRT AND GET WET!

Female ejaculation continues to be a controversial and often misunderstood topic. Reports about it could be found in western literature, which dates back to the 16th and 17th century, but the subject became popular only in the late 70s of the 20th century. Various studies claim that anywhere from 10% to 60% of all women have experienced ejaculation, but since the methods of these studies and the definition of female ejaculation vary, it is still unclear what the approximate number is. However, one fact is certain: it is far more common that most people believe and is perfectly normal and often enjoyable experience.

What Is Female Ejaculation?

The definitions vary, but the most widely accepted one defines the phenomena as expulsion of clear fluid through or around the urethra, which happens before or during an orgasm.

The characteristics of the fluid are still debated, but even though it is released from the area of the urethra, most believe that it is not urine. Establishing its character is not an easy task and often, different studies report different results on this subject as well. The most promising results are retrieved from females, who agree to abstain from sex and from whom the ejaculation fluid is examined by using their urine as a control sample. The ejaculated fluid is clear, odorless, and has taste, which much like the semen that men ejaculate, depends on the person's diet.

Most women, who experience ejaculation, report it as very enjoyable and at times, even better than the best orgasm that they have ever had, however, there are great member of females, who are reluctant to let their partners see them eject fluids. Apart from the stigma, attached to this phenomenon, there are great many myths that people still believe in even today: it should be noted that the fluid does not prevent or help women get pregnant and it does not provide additional lubrication since it has similar consistency to water. Most women report that they are far more likely to ejaculate when they or their partners stimulate them with fingers rather during intercourse, although the latter is still possible.

The Mechanism

Understanding how to bring a woman to the most fulfilling and powerful orgasm possible is a combination of a number of elements. Knowledge of female anatomy, understanding of the mechanism to stimulate her effectively as well as employing the best techniques to achieve this. However, even with all of these present a woman still has to have the right mindset or open-mindedness in order to achieve a full body orgasm.

It is up to you as her partner to enable her to feel comfortable enough to 'let go' and allow herself to be engulfed by this type of climax including ejaculation. The mechanism to achieving this is as I have already alluded to, a combination of a number of factors. If one of these is not present you and your partner may become frustrated and this will inevitably prevent her from achieving the desired effect.

The Mechanism And Tips For Achieving A Massive Female Ejaculation

- Stress - or lack of it. Ensure you and your partner have a relaxed and suitable environment in which to practice and be comfortable.

Children, telephones and TV are not conducive to providing the best environment. You have to make time for yourselves.

- Mindset - If either you or your partner are at all uncomfortable with exploring your sexuality more deeply you will find this journey fraught with frustration and disappointment. You both have to be 'open' to exploration and acceptance of the reality of achieving such a powerful orgasm.

- What is the correct technique or mechanism for achieving female ejaculation? - Once your partner is relaxed and in the right frame of mind you should have already employed some foreplay to arouse your partner. She will be more receptive to you entering her with your fingers once she has achieved a certain level of arousal. Of course, you will be able to recognise this by her body movements as well as her vagina becoming increasingly wet.

- This will allow you to enter her with two fingers. Ensure you do not have any hangnails or rough skin! Enter her vagina slowly and with fingertips upwards. Use your two fingers to move inwards and upwards and you will feel an area of her vagina that feels different to the rest. It is a patch about the size of a walnut and is slightly bumpy. This is her G-spot. Massage this firmly with your two fingers in a 'come here' motion. You should curl your fingers upwards towards you, as she becomes more aroused this area will become enlarged.

- Once you have mastered the two finger 'come hither' technique your partner should start to feel as if she may want to urinate. This is her paraurethral gland, akin to the male prostate as it becomes more stimulated. Reassure her that this will pass and if by chance she does urinate do not admonish her for it as you may never again find her receptive to any experimentation! To help ensure this does not happen it is a good idea for her to empty her bladder before foreplay begins.

- Some women enjoy the use of specially designed G-spot dildos or vibrators that can help take some of the guesswork out of actually finding the G-spot!

- Be patient. It may take some time for her to understand her own body too. Once she is close to orgasm she must 'push out' as if to urinate, not hold back as this will prevent the ejaculation. If she is too scared to push out as she starts to orgasm the ejaculate will disperse into her bladder not outwards through her urethra.

HOW TO MAKE A WOMAN EJACULATE IN RECORD TIME

- **Begins With Proper G-Spot Stimulation.**

Not all women have the ability to "squirt" when they have a vaginal orgasm. The ones who can usually have strong pc muscles. And once you learn how to do this men, you will have more sex than you can ever imagine. The #1 reason women skip sex on a nightly basis is due to the lack of pleasure they receive.

- **What You Want To Do Is Use Two Fingers To Rub Or Tap On Her G-Spot.**

It's located about two inches inside the top wall of her vagina. It's a rough patch of skin, which is flooded with blood when stimulated. When you place two fingers inside her you want to make sure you also press down on her stomach area where you will be rubbing your fingers.

- **This Places More Pressure On The G-Spot Enabling You To Arouse It More.**

While you are doing this it's best to lay on your side with your feet towards your head. This position allows you to also perform oral sex. When you combine oral sex and G-Spot stimulation, you will make this one of the most pleasurable experiences she'll ever have.

- **What You Want To Avoid Is Using Too Much Pressure Which Will Make It Hurt.**

Start using light pressure until you feel her become more aroused, then begin increasing pressure and the speed of your finger strokes. It's important to note it would be wise to have her use the bathroom before beginning this technique. If this is something new to her, she will have the sensation of needing to pee, which will go away eventually.

MALE EJACULATION

Male ejaculation seems like a pretty simple thing. However, it's a fairly complex process that only really gets investigated when problems like ED pop up. Every man should know the interworking of what needs to happen and what then occurs when men climax to have a better knowledge of self. Male ejaculation happens as the result of a series of steps involving multiple parts of the body (not just the penis!) working together. Let's break down what happens from soup to nuts (pun completely intended) when a man gets that special feeling and he wants to get it on.

Male Ejaculation Step One: Arousal

Whether he's walking down the street, at dinner with a date, or just home alone, the whole process begins at arousal. The man hears, sees, or feels something that gets Barry White to start singing in his brain, and then the brain sends a sexy telegram down the spinal cord to the sex organs which then fill with blood causing an erection.

The scrotum then pulls in toward the body as tension in the general area intensifies which is why some men feel their heartbeat in their privates when they get hard.

Fun fact: In the process of getting an erection, blood goes up to 50 times faster than its normal speed to spring a man's member to life.

All of this action is fueled by testosterone, a hormone responsible for sex drive and is produced in the testicles. While we're visiting the testicles, let's remember that's where millions of sperm are made each day and once they mature they mingle with white, protein-rich fluids which keep them safe and healthy until male ejaculation. This little man sauce is commonly known as semen.

Male Ejaculation Step Two: Plateau

This is the stage in which a man prepares to climax and can last up to two minutes. Muscle tension in the genitals increases even more and spontaneous body movements, predominantly in the pelvis, begin to take over. A man's heart rate also surges to 150 to 175 beats per minute. Pre-cum, a clear fluid, may also make an appearance from the head of the penis.

This is not only signals that arousal is high and climax is nearing, but biologically changes the pH balance of the urethra to improve sperm survival.

This stage is commonly identified by phrases like "Don't stop," and praise to a higher universal being.

Male Ejaculation Step Three: Climax or Orgasm

There are two parts to orgasm. The first is emission and the second is ejaculation. In emission, a man reaches what can only be known as "ejaculatory inevitability," and known colloquially as the point of no return. Semen has made its way up the urethra and is ready to meet the world. Male ejaculation happens in a series of intense contractions in both the penile muscles and at the base of the anus. Involuntary thrusting has also been known to happen in this stage. At the end of this, the nerves in the penis send a love note back to the brain telling it to feel pleasure.

Male Ejaculation Step Four: Resolution and Refraction

Now that the confetti has been thrown the party starts to die down.

The penis empties of blood and the erection retreats. Tension fades which causes many men to feel sleepy or at minimum, a little drowsy and looking for a nap. After resolution, men enter a period of time called the refractory period in which the penis calms and cannot be roused for a second round for a bit. The refractory period can last a few minutes to nearly an entire day depending on age and health.

Fun Fact: Women can experience multiple orgasms and still stay aroused and don't have a refractory period. That's something to consider when preparing for amore.

PREMATURE EJACULATION

Premature ejaculation is explained as a condition wherein a person is unable to delay ejaculation to a point when it is mutually desirable for both the partners. That means ejaculation occurs before a man wants it to happen. Some men ejaculate during foreplay while some do so at the very entry itself.

But few men feel that 5 or 10 minutes time to have orgasm is not enough and they feel that this is also premature ejaculation. This suggests premature ejaculation is most likely psychological in origin than physiological. The exact cause of premature ejaculation is still unknown.

Ayurveda has said Kshiprumunchati Shukram....... this means the person will have Premature ejaculation when vata in his body aggravates and leads to a very quick ejaculation of shukra (semen).

The Probable Causes For Premature Ejaculation:

- Anxiety during the first experience of sex. Some men will develop a longer-term anxiety toward sex, which can cause a prolonged experience with premature ejaculation.

- A long period of abstinence from sex.

- Younger men tend to ejaculate more quickly than older men, as experience seems to be associated with ejaculatory control.

- Depression or anxiety about poor sexual performance
- Anxiety due to anticipation of Rejection by partner.
- Anticipation of failure to satisfy his partner
- Anticipation of pain
- Adverse experiences with sex in childhood
- Religious beliefs
- Financial burdens
- Job stress
- Relationship problems
- Side effects of some prescription drugs

Apart from psychological causes, some physiological causes like inflammation of prostate gland or spinal chord problems may cause premature ejaculation.

HOW TO STOP PREMATURE EJACULATING

If you do not know how to stop premature ejaculating, sex can be a nightmare and the most embarrassing experience in your life. To stop the nightmare, you must learn how to stop premature ejaculating and say no to any more nightmares.

These are some of the easiest ways on how to stop premature ejaculating.

FIRST, USE CONDOM

When you have sex, you will feel an intense pleasure on your penis. This pleasure will lead you to the point of no return earlier than you expected or desired if you are not strong enough to control your ejaculation. To stop premature ejaculation, you need to reduce the pleasure that your penis is going through during sex. The easiest way is by wearing a condom.

Condom acts as the "mitigating medium" between the vagina and your penis. This could reduce the sensational pleasure during sex. This will enable you to last longer in bed and ejaculate only when you are ready.

SECOND, MASTURBATE PROPERLY

One of the uncommon answers to the question of how to stop premature ejaculating is "through proper masturbation".

There are 2 approaches to this method.

The easiest one is to masturbate and allow yourself to ejaculate half an hour before the actual sex. After you have had your first ejaculation, you will be able to withhold the subsequent ejaculation for a longer time during sex. That will help preventing premature ejaculation and enable you to last longer in bed.

Another approach is by doing a masturbating exercise on a regular basis to stop premature ejaculating. This exercise is known as "rub and stop" exercise.

In this exercise, you start masturbating by rubbing (or get your partner to masturbate) your penis until you feel highly stimulated and nearly ejaculate.

But right before you ejaculate, stop rubbing or masturbating and allow the stimulation to soften down. Repeat the "rub and stop" exercise for a few times before finally allowing ejaculation to take place.

How To Stop Premature Ejaculating Through This Exercise?

Well, the theory is very simple.

You would not be able to control something which you do not know. What this exercise does is to help you recognize the intense feeling or stimulation that leads to ejaculation.

Once you "know" and "are aware" how it feels right before ejaculation, you then take steps to stop that "feeling" from leading you to ejaculation before it is too late. That is why you are required to stop rubbing or masturbating when you feel that the ejaculation is nearing.

During real sex, you will be able to last longer in bed using the same approach -

- **A.** Thrust until you are nearing the point of no return

- **B.** Stop to let the feeling fade away and the stimulation to soft down

C. Thrust again

D. When you are ready, only you allow ejaculation to take place

THIRD, SLOW DOWN YOUR BREATHS

Slow down your breath is another way on how to stop premature ejaculating.

Breathing is something we do unconsciously with little knowledge that a wrong breathing method can actually lead to premature ejaculation.

If you notice, during sex, one tends to get very excited and highly stimulated. During that state, one's heart beats faster than ever and breathes fast and shallowly.

The problem is, when you breathe fast, the blood pumps in a fast mode as well causing a great amount of blood gushing towards your penis. This will lead to early ejaculation.

So, the key is to breathe slowly and deeply during sex. That will put stimulation and ejaculation at bay until you are ready.

CHAPTER TWO

SUBMISSIVE MINDSET TOWARDS A BETTER SEX

THE ACT OF SEXUALLY SUBMISSIVE

"Bad boys" make the best lovers. The idea of "bad boys" excites girls and women just like "bad girls" excite you. While you're thinking of some curvy girl ready to act on her hot carnal desires, your wife has in her imagination some big guy who knows how to dominate a woman way beyond bondage for beginners.

But if she's a shy, submissive girl she will not tell you such fantasies just like you're not going to tell her about the dirty things in YOUR mind during intimate moments together. To be fair, as a shy and submissive wife she may even hide the detail of her fantasies from herself. Her parents likely trained her just as you would train your own daughters - be respectable, be quiet, be NICE. Right?

You wouldn't want some rough, sexually over-active biker chick as your wife. And your submissive girl doesn't want a brute as a husband.

But you want more sizzle.

If she could say it out loud, she wants more sizzle too.

And the steak.

Most men try to get more sex in a two basic ways.

One way is to simply make demands of your wife. As you probably know from bitter experience, simply asking for sex is not a way that works with a woman whose sexual training has been one of ignoring her own sexual needs and desires. She will likely feel pressured and "bad".

Another way to try for more sex is to gently suggest and hint. Sometimes this can be by piling on the romance. In the man's mind, the romance is like foreplay - you romance her with flowers and dinner and a walk in the moonlight and she gives you a night of good sex. Of course, for a submissive woman, the romance IS as far as she can imagine. She has been trained long and hard by her parents and society to AVOID thinking about any pulsing between her legs so she likes the romance for its own sake! You lose. At other times suggestions and hints can be suggestive touches and comments that would get you going if she did them to you. But again, if her sexual training has been to suppress her desires she'll think you're being a pain in the butt or simply crude.

But There Is Another Way To Get The Sex You Need: Learn How To Train A Submissive Female.

The things you can do in training is much the same as you'd train a child or an athlete: pick your small target, induce her to reach the goal, reward her emotionally and physically.

Then set the bar higher. When training your submissive wife you're also training yourself in how to sexually dominate your wife. Sure there should be some basic beginner's bondage. But these are all the big things that can come later. Simple truth is that you don't need to master bondage, domination, sadomasochism, or female slave training to sexually dominate your wife.

In the short term, what you need to do is to find ways of getting your submissive wife to express her desires to you without having to say them in words. Then you can take her step by step towards living out her unstated fantasies.

Each of these is the small steps you need to give her and the excitement she'll get from living out those unstated fantasies will be a big reward each time.

When you have sex with your wife in the so-called "missionary position" (her on her back and you on top), how often does she place her hands above her head? Placing her hands there is not to keep them out of the way.

She's got a fantasy in her mind of being controlled - perhaps wrists held by the man taking her, or maybe her hands are tied up so that she can't resist. If you were wanting to explore bondage for beginners that would be a good way to start - a silk scarf or even a dressing gown belt - no fancy knots, just something wound around her wrists (not too tight to scare her!) and watch the expression on her face and feel the sudden surge of her excitement!

The truth is that most emotionally healthy women are sexually submissive. This means that they want men who TAKE CONTROL and LEAD THEM.

Not what we usually hear in mainstream men's sex advice, right?

But this is the truth about women and sex.

So, women what sexually dominant men in the bedroom. Please take note of that last sentence very carefully when it says 'in the bedroom'. Men who control their women outside the bedroom are insecure, sad, pathetic men who prey on insecure women.

But in the bedroom -- women want their man to be in charge.

They want to follow his lead.

They want to do as they are told.

For you to act like this with your woman and have her respond favorably, you must command respect and your woman must take you seriously.

With respect, you are in a position to unleash your woman's wildly sexual side.

Here is how you unleash your woman's wildly sexual side and get everything you want in the bedroom and totally SEXUALLY SATISFY her in the process:

First off, you instigate the sex. You never ask or beg for sex.

Next, you take control and you lead her through each and every sexual experience that you share together.

Then you start doing things that are considered NAUGHTY and TABOO in the bedroom because women love to 'get naughty'. You grab her hair and talk dirty whilst you are doing it 'doggy-style'. You tell her when to come. You spank her ass. You generally get downright nasty.

And she will love it.

Listen up...

Women want to be ravaged by their men.

And do you know what they want most of all?

They want earth shattering, mind-blowing, knee trembling ORGASMS. And they don't just want the usual clitoral orgasms -- they want vaginal, multiple, anal and squirting orgasms too.

HOW TO MAKE HER GENUINELY SUBMISSIVE

Have A Genuine Desire To Satisfy Her, And Then Do It.

I've said this before, I'll say it again, and probably again in the future: If you actually take the time and effort to make sure that she has an orgasm before you, she would be willing to do whatever you want her to.

You want to tie her up? You want to pull her hair? Spank her? Choke her?

Chances are that you can do all of those things as long as you ensure that she has her orgasm first. (And I'm talking about a real, hair-raising, toe-curling, and earth-shaking orgasm)

There is nothing more powerful than a sexually satisfied woman.

"Tread Softly" And Check For Feedback

If you've never slept with your partner before, you probably don't want to bring out the whips and the chains just yet. If she's letting you spank her, it probably doesn't mean that she wants you to stick your finger in her butt.

Whatever you want to try, you have to "test" the idea first by doing a very light version of the idea, and then check for her reaction to see if you should continue or not.

For example, if you want to ultimately stick a vibrator in her butt you have to first rub your finger across her anus while you're having sex to see how she reacts to it. If she squirms and says, "No!" then you know that you probably shouldn't continue.

But if she doesn't shut you down right away, then you can continue to stroke it. Then slowly and gently begin to slide your finger in only up to the first knuckle. Then you stop here and continue your vaginal stroke.

If she is enjoying it, you'll either hear her moans intensify or you'll actually feel lubrication coming from her anus. This can be a sign that you can push your finger deeper. But if you want to be even more careful, you can just ask her how she likes it. This can apply to anything... pulling her hair, tying her up, using toys, etc.

SEX POSITION

There are many reasons to try new sex positions which step beyond the boundary of what you may be used to. The first is sexual excitement. By trying new positions, you can add a new level of sexual excitement to any sexual relationship.

Remember, it is not necessary that you perform sex only in one position every time you have sex. It is said that variety is the spice of life and it also applies to sex as well. In this article, we discuss some better sex positions so that you can practice the same with your partner. It is very necessary that you be careful while experimenting with a new position. You or your partner may not be comfortable with a new position or may be feeling hurt. It is recommended that you stop performing the act immediately.

Four Reasons You Ought To Bring In Some Fun Sex Positions To Your Sex Life

1. **It Can Put The Spice Back In A Relationship.**

Adding fun to sex is a really good cure to monotony in the relationship. And just what better method to add fun into sex than to try creative and new positions? You see, when you are doing the same things repeatedly, sex comes to be a routine. If sex becomes routine, it is easy for boredom to set in. When you let an unfulfilling sex life rule your relationship, you will find yourselves drifting away from each other. Adding fun to sex is a resolution that can stop boredom and sustain the intimacy in your relationship.

2. **It Can Accentuate Your Climax.**

If you want to experience this yourself or make your partner orgasm and you are finding it challenging with your usual sexual encounters, then you might just wish to try a few new fun sex positions.

These positions are useful in making your partner, in particular when it comes to the female, reach a climax and have an incredible orgasm. Position matters whenever it comes to bringing your partner to bliss. By tweaking some of your basic sex positions the fun can really kick off. Using precise targeting of the g-spot by means of the right positions, you and your partner can expect to have the most extraordinary sex ever.

3. It May Reduce Your Stress.

Being stuck in a sex routine could add to a stressful relationship. It would not do you or your loved one any good to have sex when either of you feels that it is an obligation. This turns into a different story with fun sex positions. By breaking the dullness of sex, these sort of positions may add exhilaration and bliss to intercourse.

When you look forward to undertaking something that provides you with so much pleasure, it can help your body produce and release hormones that can minimize your stress levels. If you want to ease any tension in your relationship and restore the spice, try and deviate from your typical sex positions and try out some fresh and unfamiliar ones.

4. Live A Much Longer Life.

With the three previous reasons, trying fun sex positions will help you as well as your partner live a longer life. Statistics reveal that sex in itself has the potential to strengthen your body's natural protection against illnesses and diseases. Added to this are the benefits you can get from fun and laughter such as healing and delaying the aging process.

These four are good justifications for you to see sex from a different point of view. By doing this, you can open yourselves to numerous positions that may bring more pleasure and gratification to you and your partner. Perhaps it's time you engage and benefit from some fun sex positions?

THE FOLLOWING IS A LIST OF DIFFERENT SEX POSITIONS YOU COULD EXPERIMENT

1. Man on top

This is one of the most common, bread and butter sex position for most couples. In this position, man gets on top of the women and they come face to face. Majority of the couples start their first sexual act with this position. However, nowadays, people consider this position to be old fashioned and look for better sex positions.

2. Woman On Top

Woman on top is the most delightful sexual position enjoyed by almost all men and women alike. This is one of the more preferable positions today.

For a man, it provides the opportunity to lie back and enjoy the ride! For a woman, it provides the opportunity to be sexually assertive while she gets exactly the stimulation and arousal she needs to reach orgasm. It is a very powerful sexual position!

3. Sitting

Sitting sex positions tend to be restful and gentle. A couple can engage with each other emotionally. She may wish to ride him, either gently or fast, though she may get tired quite quickly if her leg muscles are not used to the exercise. A big advantage of sex in the sitting position is that the couple can rest whenever they wish, perhaps kissing and cuddling until they are ready to resume thrusting. It is also easy to switch from sitting sex to just about any other position.

4. Standing

This is one of the most difficult positions as both the partners are standing.

Penetration may become difficult and since most of the women are shorter than their partners, they will have to stand on the stool to get into a better position. The partners may hold each other during the act to get a better grip.

5. Side-by-Side

In this case, the partners lie on their sides on the bed. The only disadvantage in this position is that one partner has to keep his legs above the legs of the other partner and as a result, the other partner may get cramps after a while.

6. Rear Entry

This is the most sexual of all sex positions. In this case, the man inserts his penis from the rear end. This means the woman has to kneel on her knees and then the man enters from the rear.

7. Enhanced Missionary Position

Missionary position is believed to be a common and old style of sex. This is true also but although of its old origin, yet it still bears the most stimulating and pleasurable features that will allow you both to enjoy sex. For this purpose, you need to add some new enhancement in it but to a little extent.

You need to lay her on the bed and get yourself up to her (at the top). Deviating from the normal style, you should open her legs wider. Do remember that in this enhanced missionary position, you do not need to hold her legs; however, you need to punch on her passionately. This position will make her hips more moving and the penetration will go deeper than any other sexual position. In this way, you can really please your woman in bed.

8. Doggy-style

Well, Doggy-style position is a well-known and tested position to please women inefficient way. This position also gives the woman a powerful orgasm quite earlier and in a raunchy way.

This is different and one of the most distinct sex positions as this is used by many creatures other than the human beings on this earth. This sex position is also suggested to the men who want to calm down their extra sexual excitement and hence they can last longer in bed also.

9. Lying Face Down

Lying face down is a superb sex position to have an unforgettable orgasm for both partners. In this position, the man is on top and he penetrates from the back. The woman lays on bed with her face in downward direction. She lifts her butts upward in front of man and usually, she doesn't open her legs. This position is good for you to please your woman in bed as the legs of your woman remain closed and you can enjoy more stimulation because there is more friction with woman's legs closed.

10. Cowboy Sex Position

If you like to spice things up in the bedroom with a little role reversal then the cowboy is one of those positions for lovemaking that will appeal to those who like to do things a little different.

This position is where the woman lays on her back and the man sits on top. It's for men who like the feeling of trapping their lady underneath to maintain control. It should be noted though that it can be difficult for your guy to dock... and when he does, it will only permit for shallow penetration. However, the vaginal tightness created by your closed legs will please him but some clitoral stimulation for you may be required.

11. The Ambush

The ambush is one of those making love positions that can feel a bit like a drunken romp but some will find it hot, if not a little amusing.

Laying flat on your back with your legs over your head, he penetrates you while laying across your lower body in the opposite direction. It's one of those weird sex positions that for the right couple can either be a big hit or a definite miss.

12. The Hangman

If you're wondering what are good sex positions to create a bit of swinging motion, then The Hungman is a good place to start. It's where he hangs from a rail above and supports his legs on a chair. You straddle over his legs and slide down on to his cock. If he then has good upper body strength you can attempt to swing back and forth.

13. The Motion of the Ocean

This is another one of those weird sex positions that will require a bit of creative flair and a touch on finesse. He sits on a rocking chair and you sit on him with your back to him. Holding hands you lean forward, your face almost to the ground, and you begin to rock.

14. The Rickshaw

The Rickshaw is certainly one of the most creative sex positions. It requires him to lay back on the end of the bed with his hips overhanging over the edge with his legs bent up. You stand with your back to him then lower yourself down on his cock while holding on to his feet.

15. I Want My Mummy

A reverse gender role and only for those ladies strong enough to hold their man like a child whilst leaning back up against a wall. Not for most this one definitely tops the weird sex positions guide!

16. The Wheel Barrow Sex Position

The Wheel Barrow position is definitely for the adventurous couples that love creative sex positions. Just like the 'wheelbarrow' races you had at school, this varied version has a definite naughty twist, making it for sex lovers who love to pound and be pounded!

To get into the wheelbarrow sex position, have him lift your pelvis as you grip his waist with your legs and support your upper body with your arms on the floor. It will definitely require stamina from both parties but a great advantage of this kinky position is the great angle it provides for g spot stimulation, as well as giving him a great view of your body. And if he's got good balance he can also stimulate your anus or clitoris.

When you get tired you can always go down on your forearms, almost like a rear aerial Pilates plank position to give your arms and shoulders a bit of a rest. But if you love hard and fast movements, this is one of the best deep penetration positions that will appeal to those who like it rough.

17. Dancer Position:

Dancer Sex Position is definitely one of the most advanced sex positions because there are very few adult women who will actually be able to get into it. This tricky position requires excellent flexibility and it also helps if you are of a similar height to your partner.

To get into the dancer sex position, stand face forward, lift one leg right up over his shoulder and hold on around his waist or shoulders. Or as a variation, you can also just wrap your leg around his waist and balance on your tippy toe as he supports your weight.

Dancer sex position is fantastic for shower sex. if your man has good quad strength, he can even bounce you up and down while having the freedom to either grab on to your rear or kiss and caress you by pinning you up against the wall.

18. Viennese Oyster

The Viennese Oyster is certainly one of the most creative positions that definitely requires some limbering up, but if you're flexible enough to do it, the rewards are plenty!

To get into the Viennese Oyster position, lay back and lift both legs behind your ears giving the visual presentation of an oyster. This may take some time getting in to as well as some practice to maintain but being one of hardest and most advanced sex positions, it's definitely worth the time you put into preparing for it

If you can do it, it's the outright exposure and feeling of naughtiness that makes the Viennese Oyster so erotic. From this position, he can lick and suck your lady zone and can further arouse you by inserting fingers into your vagina or anus or both. Only when you are moaning for more should he penetrate and if he thrusts in hard at an upward angle this is one of the best deep penetration positions to maximize your chance of hitting your g spot.

19. The Dragon Position

In this sex position, the woman stretches out onto her stomach, with her legs slightly apart, placing a few pillows underneath her pelvis to raise her buttocks. Her partner can then easily penetrate her by stretching over on top of her. It's a great alternative to traditional rear entry position, offering deep penetration and relief to people who suffer from knee problems.

20. The Butterfly Position

This is one of the best sex positions for women because it positions the man in such a way as to give easy access to her g-spot.

So no matter how he moves, her favorite pleasure spots will always be stimulated. In this position, the woman lies on her back, while the man elevates her hips with his arms to align both of their genitals. He can then move, freely in all directions, alternating as he watches her growing sexual desire

21. Reverse Cowgirl Position

In this sex position, the woman faces her partner's feet while she sits astride him. She has the control in this position, which allows her the freedom to move at the rate and speed that fills her to brink of pleasure. Her man, laying beneath her can either relax and enjoy the rear view or move in unison with her.

22. LeapFrog Position

Similar to the rear entry position, but instead of being on all fours, the woman lowers her torso onto the bed, while her partner penetrates her on his knees or squatting over her. This is an extremely submissive position for women, which some might find to be extremely arousing. But it's really a matter of preference.

23. Spoon Split Position

This sex position is a favorite by many women because it's very intimate, but also very stimulating. To perform the Spoon Split, both partners lie on their side, with the man aligning himself behind his woman. With one hand, he grasps her top leg and wraps it over his own. While he thrusts deeply, he can freely stimulate her clitoris and massage her breasts.

MISTAKES MOST PEOPLE MAKE WHEN MAINTAINING THE BEST SEX POSITIONS

Most men face a common challenge when they have to decide on the best sex positions when in bed with their girl. Most of them simply fear that their girl might get bored if they repeat the same sex position every time they make love. Always keep in mind that same old always produces boring results. So they generally wonder what the best sex positions are when making love?

So, one of the best ways is to try and explain what you are not supposed to do when making sex. Most people try imitating positions they see in a number of porn movies. This is one of the main reasons why most men fail when having sex. Most inexperienced men feel the need of looking porn movies before having sex, to satisfy their girl. They just feel that porn is best as they see some of the best studs banging sexy boards..... This is what they can be named! Always keep in mind that porn movies use sex positions so viewers can see it and enjoy it. This certainly does not make it Best Positions for you!

You have to keep in mind that one of the worst sex positions is when women place her ankles on your shoulders as she might feel the pain when having sex. This is also one of the best positions that might put in all the pleasure in your sex life. Second point to keep in mind is that you just don't have to try too hard to keep your weight away from your girl. Sex is definitely one way in which women can get closer to her man. So if you lean on her to maintain best positions ten she might love having it with you.

So, next time when you try having sex with her, please try gaining more weight so she can feel it. When having sex, most women like when she feels the weight of her man on her body. Try placing enough weight so after intercourse she might, in fact, tell you that she could feel being smushed. Avoid grinding her pubic bone for a longer period of time as it might pain her.

Always keep in mind that in case your women is on top of you, avoid letting her do entire job. Sex is generally considered as a passive act for most women. So in case you are motionless then she might, in fact, loose all interest in having it with you. Never destroy the entire purpose of having sex with your girl. Maintaining one of the Best Sex Positions is possible if both of you are having equal interest in it.

PENIS HEALTH THROUGH POST-SEX HYGIENE

After a man enjoys a robust play session with their favorite partner (or a brand new one!), he probably just wants to roll over, smile and go to sleep for a while. But when it comes to good penis care, that's actually the last thing he needs to do. Hygiene is vitally important when it comes to penis health, and that includes good hygiene practices after his sexual desire is sated.

Post-Sex Hygiene Tips

When a guy gets it on, there are plenty of bodily fluids that come into play. But there are also other things that might linger on the penis, such as the residue from spermicide in a condom, lube that might have been employed during the course of play - and depending upon how adventurous a couple gets, there could even be body paint or juice from pieces of fruit!

Needless to say, leaving these things on the penis for a long while is not a good idea. A man who sleeps for even a few hours with these fluids on his penis and surrounding area could easily wake up to a sore, red, irritated penis - and that doesn't bode well for a round two with that deserving partner.

With that in mind, there are some tips a man can look to for proper post-sex hygiene.

1. Keep Tissues Near The Bed.

The last thing a man wants to do is ruin the afterglow. But on the other hand, he doesn't want to let things get all sticky down there. A good compromise is reaching for a tissue on the bedside table to wipe away most of the fluids and residue on his penis. This buys some time before he gets into the shower.

2. Use Baby Wipes.

A man who is getting it on somewhere other than the bedroom - say, on a camping trip - might not have easy access to a shower or sink.

In that case, baby wipes to the rescue! These handy little wipes are great for anything, so a guy should keep them around just in case, but they are great for the post-sex cleanup, too.

3. Do A quick Rinse.

Sometimes a man doesn't want to get a full shower right after he's enjoyed his partner - especially if she is lying in bed waiting on his return. A quick trip to the bathroom to rinse off the penis and surrounding area can be a great way to keep things clean but not keep an eager partner waiting for too long.

4. Shower Together.

A guy who wants to get even more action could suggest they both shower together. This allows everyone to get squeaky clean, provides plenty of visual stimulation and could even get him ready for another round.

5. Watch For Redness.

Right after sex is a great time to look for any issues with the penis, especially redness, soreness and swelling. That's because many men have adverse reactions to the spermicide, lubrication or condoms themselves, and often the problem shows up immediately after using those items.

6. Use An Excellent Penis Health Crème.

Right after his shower, a man can reach for a great penis health crème. This will help ensure that his penis has plenty of hydration and all the topical ingredients it needs to stay in tip-top shape.

HYGIENE RULES FOR AN HEALTHY VAGINA

The vagina is a sensitive area, and keeping it healthy should be a concern for all women. There is a delicate balance of healthy bacteria in the vagina, and these levels can be easily disrupted. It is also normal for there to be a small amount of discharge which helps to keep the vaginal area clean and free from harmful bacteria. When the PH level in the vaginal area is disrupted, many women experience irritation, burning, and even an infection. Here are some tips for woman to follow that will help them keep their vaginas healthy and the PH level balanced.

Hygiene Rules for a Healthy Vagina

These simple tips can help your vaginal area stay healthy, so you can enjoy satisfying and pleasurable sex life. Any woman who experiences any irritation or pain in her vaginal area should speak with her health care provider immediately to determine the cause and appropriate treatment.

1. Try to Refrain from Douching.

Many women grew up hearing that it was necessary to douche to avoid feminine vaginal odour and to keep their areas clean. The harsh chemicals and perfumes in many of the available douches can actually upset the delicate PH balance and cause vaginal irritation and even odour. Instead of trying to mask vaginal odour with a scented douche, white or apple cider vinegar can be used to cleanse the vaginal area without upsetting the PH balance or harming the beneficial bacteria.

2. Eating Healthy is Important.

What a woman eats is not only important for her appearance and weight, but it can also affect the health of her vagina. Many researchers recommend adding yogurt to the diet to help promote the growth of health bacteria. Drinking plenty of water can also help to flush harmful toxins out of the body that could cause vaginal problems. Some women have also found that cranberries can also improve vaginal health along with soy products.

3. Always Practice Safe Sex.

Sexually transmitted diseases are a common and preventable problem that can cause a woman to experience pain, discomfort, and irritation in her vaginal area. While some sexually transmitted diseases can be treated with antibiotics, there is no cure for HIV or genital herpes. Simply wearing a condom can prevent the transfer of STDs. It is also important to remember to change condoms during intercourse if both anal and vaginal penetration is performed. Bacteria located in the anus can cause problems with the vaginal PH levels.

4. Treat Infections as Soon as They Appear.

Almost all women will experience yeast or bacterial infection in their vaginal area at least once in their lives. These infections can occur without exposure to a sexually transmitted disease and can be caused by a number of different factors. These infections can normally be cleared up with an antibiotic or anti-fungal ointment and should be treated by a health care professional.

5. Lubrication is Important.

Not only is vaginal dryness uncomfortable during intercourse for a woman, but it can also be painful for her partner. For occasional cases of vaginal dryness, a lubricant or lotion can be topically applied. This can help to prevent irritation and tearing on the vaginal lining that can result in a painful infection. One thing to remember is to avoid greasy or oil-based lubricating products since they can harm the beneficial bacteria in the vagina.

6. Clothing Can Cause Vaginal Problems.

Yeast and some bacterial infections can be caused by wearing tight clothing. Clothing does not let air flow around the vagina, can cause harmful bacteria to grow. To keep this area cool and moist, women should try to wear loosely fitting cotton underwear and avoid synthetic fabrics. It is also important to not wear damp swimsuits or spandex workout clothing for long periods of time.

7. Hygiene is Always Important.

The best way to keep your vagina healthy is to follow basic hygiene rules.

Always wash gently with warm water, and avoid harsh chemicals or fragrances. Always change sanitary pads and tampons regularly, and avoid wiping towards the vagina after a bowel movement.

CONCLUSION

Having a good sex life is usually a good indicator of the health of your marriage. If your sex life is not healthy, what can you do about it? Men are usually the ones that complain that they do not get enough sex, but not always. Sometimes it is the other way around. If your husband is not interested in sex, he may be low in testosterone levels and that is easily checked by going to the doctor and getting cream. If a woman is not interested in sex her estrogen could be low and she can also have her levels checked.

If you are not having good sex and your hormone levels are normal, then talk about what else may be the problem. Sometimes the way we are brought up can have an influence on the way we see sex. If we see it as being dirty or shameful, then we are not going to enjoy sex. It can be an indication that we have not matured emotionally into adulthood and we subconsciously see ourselves as children and children do not have sex. You still see yourself under the authority of your parents. This occurs when your family is enmeshed and your individuality has never been affirmed.

Your relationship may not feel safe and if there is emotional, verbal or physical abuse then you will not enjoy sex with an abusive spouse. Don't be afraid to ask for help from other safe people who care about you and can give you tools to set boundaries. If you have children, it is not healthy for them to see you being abused.

When we do not feel emotionally safe with our spouse, sex is going to be the last thing we want. Healthy communication and learning how to validate one another and love and respect each other is essential in enjoying good sex. Good sex does not happen like it does in the movies. It just does not work that way. It takes time and effort to build a good sex life, just like anything else that is worthwhile.

Educate yourself about what a good sex life looks like and communicate with your spouse and ask what their needs are and what you can do to make it better. Men enjoy seeing their wives look nice and attractive. They are stimulated by site. They get turned on quickly. Women are slower and they need love-making to start in the morning with kindness and love. Husbands can express their love by knowing their wife's love language and give her that throughout the day. When she feels loved and appreciated she will have more time for sex.

CPSIA information can be obtained
at www.ICGtesting.com
Printed in the USA
BVHW042350040621
608823BV00012B/3393

9 781803 041216